Asha

Linda Chapman lives in Leicestershire with her family and two dogs. When she is not writing, she spends her time looking after her three children, reading, talking to people about writing, and horse riding whenever she can.

You can find out more about Linda on her websites at *lindachapman.co.uk* and *lindachapmanauthor.co.uk*

Books by Linda Chapman

BRIGHT LIGHTS
CENTRE STAGE
MY SECRET UNICORN series
NOT QUITE A MERMAID series
SKATING SCHOOL series
SKY HORSES series
STARDUST series
UNICORN SCHOOL series

Skating

Silver Skate Surprise

School

Linda Chapman

Illustrated by Nellie Ryan

PUFFIN

Madame Letsworth's Magic Ice-Skating Academy

FROST FAIRIES

MOLLY   HANNAH   EMILY   TILDA   ALICE

ICE OWLS

AMANDA   ZOE   HEATHER   TASHA   OLIVIA

SNOW FOXES

CAMILLA   TESS   CLARE   HELENA

To Lee Weatherly for reading through this book, for understanding what I was trying to do, and for all the ideas and encouragement throughout the whole series. Thank you!

PUFFIN BOOKS

Published by the Penguin Group
Penguin Books Ltd, 80 Strand, London WC2R ORL, England
Penguin Group (USA) Inc., 375 Hudson Street, New York, New York 10014, USA
Penguin Group (Canada), 90 Eglinton Avenue East, Suite 700, Toronto, Ontario, Canada M4P 2Y3
(a division of Pearson Penguin Canada Inc.)
Penguin Ireland, 25 St Stephen's Green, Dublin 2, Ireland (a division of Penguin Books Ltd)
Penguin Group (Australia), 250 Camberwell Road, Camberwell, Victoria 3124, Australia
(a division of Pearson Australia Group Pty Ltd)
Penguin Books India Pvt Ltd, 11 Community Centre, Panchsheel Park, New Delhi – 110 017, India
Penguin Group (NZ), 67 Apollo Drive, Rosedale, North Shore 0632, New Zealand
(a division of Pearson New Zealand Ltd)
Penguin Books (South Africa) (Pty) Ltd, 24 Sturdee Avenue, Rosebank, Johannesburg 2196, South Africa

Penguin Books Ltd, Registered Offices: 80 Strand, London WC2R ORL, England

puffinbooks.com

First published 2010
1

Text copyright © Linda Chapman, 2010
Illustrations copyright © Nellie Ryan, 2010
All rights reserved

The moral right of the author and illustrator has been asserted

Set in 15/22 pt Bembo
Typeset by Palimpsest Book Production Limited, Grangemouth, Stirlingshire
Made and printed in England by Clays Ltd, St Ives plc

Except in the United States of America, this book is sold subject to the condition that it shall not, by way of trade or otherwise, be lent, re-sold, hired out, or otherwise circulated without the publisher's prior consent in any form of binding or cover other than that in which it is published and without a similar condition including this condition being imposed on the subsequent purchaser

British Library Cataloguing in Publication Data
A CIP catalogue record for this book is available from the British Library

ISBN: 978-0-141-32638-2

www.greenpenguin.co.uk

Penguin Books is committed to a sustainable future
for our business, our readers and our planet.
The book in your hands is made from paper
certified by the Forest Stewardship Council.

Contents

In the Magic Land of Ice and Winter . . . 1

1. Scurrying Snowballs 5

2. The Lulling Dance 19

3. A Brilliant Idea 29

4. Plans and Preparations 41

5. Midnight Magic 55

6. The Final Competition 69

7. The Shortlist 79

8. The Ice Princess 89

9. Going Home 107

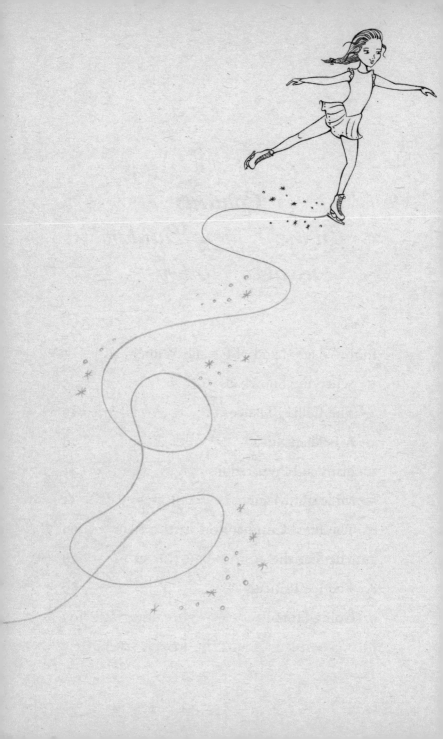

In the Magic Land of Ice and Winter . . .

Things were getting worse. A blanket of snow still covered the fields and meadows, towns and villages, and the frozen lakes on the lower slopes of the mountains still glittered in the pale sun. But up on the high peaks the snow and ice were melting.

Buds on the trees were breaking out into green leaves and the frozen rivers that ran down the craggy slopes were turning to water. Every so often an avalanche of softened snow and rocks would crash down the mountains with a muffled roar.

The ice sylphs who lived in the lower reaches of the land were very worried. Up in the mountains, a fire dragon had curled around one of the highest peaks, jets of fire streaming out of its mouth

with every breath as it rested. The sylphs knew they had to persuade it to move before it did any more damage. But to do that they needed an Ice Princess.

In the Magic Ice-skating Academy, three of the teachers were looking at a list of girls' names.

'Which girl will it be?' Madame Li, one of the ice-skating teachers, wondered.

Monsieur Carvallio, a tall, dark ice sylph, studied the list. 'Nearly all of them are now good enough at skating to be the Ice Princess and perform the Lulling Dance for us.'

'But the Ice Princess needs to be more than just a good ice-skater,' Madame Letsworth, the headteacher, reminded them. 'She must be a certain type of

person to make the magic in the dance work.'

'We have to choose well,' agreed Madame Li.

Madame Letsworth's gaze ran over the names. She had a feeling she knew which girl it might be, but there was still time for one of the other girls to surprise her. In a week's time the teachers would make their decision. Who was it going to be?

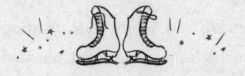

Chapter One
Scurrying Snowballs

Emily, Hannah and Molly swished
across the snow on their skis, past trees
sparkling with icicles. Emily pushed
first one pole and then the other, her
brown hair blowing back from her face.
She'd never been cross-country skiing
before she came to the Land of Ice and
Winter. But then she'd never driven
a sledge pulled by huskies, talked to

an ice dragon or held a frost fairy
either!

Hannah and Molly were chatting.
Hannah's long blonde hair was tied in a
ponytail and Molly's black hair was held
back by a hairband. The three of them
had become really good friends since
they had first arrived at the Ice-skating
Academy. Five weeks ago they had been
whisked away from the human world
by magic and given the opportunity to
stay in the Land of Ice and Winter for
six weeks, improving their skating,
living at the school and going to classes
together.

The ice sylphs who taught at the
school had told them that no one would
know they had gone because time passed
differently in the magic world. At the

end of their time at the Ice-skating
Academy, one of the girls would be
chosen to be the Ice Princess, a girl who
would help the ice sylphs.

Emily was very glad she had decided to
stay. She'd had a brilliant time – it had
been the best five weeks of her life. She
could hardly believe that in just a week
she, and all the others, would be going
back to their normal lives. *I know we'll*

e-mail and phone each other when we're back home, she thought. *But it won't be the same.*

'You're quiet, Em.' Hannah glanced over. 'Are you OK?'

Emily sighed. 'Just thinking about going home.'

'Well, don't,' said Molly quickly. 'We won't enjoy our last few days if we keep thinking about all of this ending on

Sunday. No talking about going home this week, OK?'

Emily and Hannah nodded.

'Let's talk about the Ice Princess instead,' Molly went on. 'Just think – whoever it is will get to see a real fire dragon!'

The girls had been told that an enormous fire dragon had landed on a mountain and that his breath was melting all the snow and the rivers, endangering the whole land. One of the girls was going to be chosen to be the Ice Princess. She would have to perform a magic ice dance in front of the dragon to try to make him fly on. If she did it successfully, she would be granted a wish as a reward.

'What would you wish for, Hannah,' asked Molly, 'if you got to be the Ice Princess?'

Hannah thought hard. 'I don't know. Maybe to be the best skater in the world – to be Olympic champion one day.'

'I'd wish for something that would give me unlimited wishes,' said Molly. 'Or if we weren't allowed that, I'd wish for loads of money so I could buy everyone everything they wanted. Then I'd get myself a massive limousine so I could visit you both all the time, and maybe a big house in the country where we could all go in the holidays. Oh, and my own ice rink and full-time coach and my own sweet shop.'

Emily giggled. 'Not much then!'

'Nope.' Molly grinned. 'Just a few little things.'

'What about you, Em?' asked Hannah.

Emily hadn't thought much about the wish. All she really wanted was to be chosen as Ice Princess and to save the land, even though it would mean skating in front of a massive dragon. 'I'm not sure. Maybe that when I'm back home I can go ice-skating lots. Though Molly's wish sounds good!'

'I wonder what the competition will be this week,' mused Hannah.

Every week the girls took part in a competition that the ice sylphs set to help them choose who would be the Ice Princess. The winner was awarded a special pair of coloured skates. Sometimes the competitions had involved ice-skating, but at other times the girls had competed outside in teams, doing things like scavenger hunts, relay races and even husky driving!

'We'll find out about this week's

competition when we get back,' Molly said. 'We know it's going to –'

'Hey, look at that!' Hannah interrupted her. She pointed at a snowball that was on top of the bank of a frozen river. It was rolling along as if it was alive.

'Oh, wow! It's a snowball mouse,' Emily exclaimed as the mouse rolled down the bank and stopped nearby.

'It's a *what*?' Molly stared at her.

'A snowball mouse,' Emily repeated. She had read lots of books about the Land of Ice and Winter and the creatures that inhabited it. 'They're just normal mice, but they have fluffy coats so they can disguise themselves as a snowball if an owl or fox comes along. I've wanted to see one for ages. They're amazing. They live in big groups. If one gets *really* scared, it squeaks

loudly and all the other snowball mice
jump on top of each other's backs until
they're in a massive ball. Then they roll
towards the predator, frightening it off.'

'That's so cool!' said Molly. She went
closer to look at the mouse, but as she
did so her ski slipped on a patch of ice
and she fell over. 'Whoa!' she gasped.

'That's so not!' Hannah said, and they
all giggled.

Emily was just about to ski over and help Molly up when there was the sound of voices. Two girls came skiing through the trees. The girl in the front was very pretty with strawberry-blonde hair.

Emily's heart sank. It was Camilla, her least favourite girl at the school, with her best friend, Tess.

Seeing Emily, Molly and Hannah, they came over. 'Oh dear, have you fallen over, Molly?' said Camilla, her eyebrows rising. 'How careless. You've obviously been hanging round with Emily for too long.'

Emily was the least experienced skater at skating school and she had fallen over a lot at first when she had been skating. She had improved really quickly, but Camilla wouldn't let her forget about it.

'That's not fair!' Molly protested.

'Emily hardly falls over now at all when she's skating!'

Camilla smiled. 'Oh, yes, silly me. I forgot. Here, let me help you up, Molly.' She held out her hand.

Looking surprised, Molly took it, but as she was halfway to her feet Camilla let go and Molly bumped back down again.

'Whoops! Sorry. My hand must have slipped,' said Camilla, grinning at Tess.

'Oh, ha, ha, very funny,' said Molly as Emily and Hannah quickly helped her to her feet.

'Well, *I* thought so,' Camilla said smugly. She and Tess started to ski off.

Then Molly's eyes fell on the snowball mouse near Camilla's feet. A mischievous grin crossed her face. Bending down, she grabbed a handful of snow and threw it at Camilla's back. It splatted against her shoulder.

Camilla gasped and swung round. 'Why . . . you . . .' Spotting the mouse, she assumed it was a ready-made snowball. She instantly swooped on him, picked him up and . . .

'*EEEEEE!*' the mouse squeaked loudly in alarm. Camilla stared in shock. There was a flurry of movement in the

bushes and out scurried about a hundred other mice.

'But . . . but . . .' stammered Camilla as they headed towards her.

Tess squealed. 'What's happening?'

The mouse, still clutched in Camilla's hand, squeaked again. The other mice jumped on each other's backs and formed a giant snowball that began to roll towards Camilla. She tried to run backwards, but it was impossible in skis and she tripped over.

'Argh!' she cried as the snowball reached her and she was suddenly covered in a blanket of white scurrying mice. They jumped on her head, ran down her arms and covered her legs and body so that only her head was poking out.

Emily, Molly and Hannah burst out laughing.

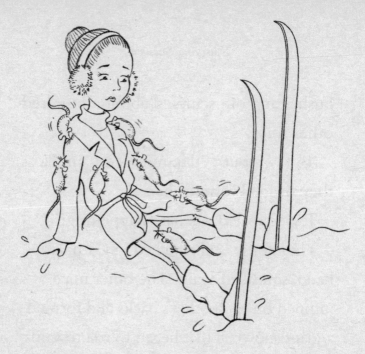

'Get them off me!' Camilla shrieked to Tess.

Molly grinned as Tess hurried forward to help. 'Oh dear, you've fallen over, Camilla. How careless of you.' She turned to Emily and Hannah. 'Come on. I want to find out about the competition.'

Chuckling together and leaving an outraged Camilla being helped up from the snow, the three of them skied away.

Chapter Two
The Lulling Dance

Half an hour later, the girls clustered
round Madame Letsworth at the side of
the ice rink. Frost fairies fluttered
through the air. They were each about
two centimetres high, with gauzy wings
and clouds of fluffy hair. The frost fairies
looked after everything at the skating
school – tidying up, doing the cooking
and keeping the ice smooth.

Emily put out her hand towards them. Two of the fairies flew over and perched on her fingers, smiling up at her and chattering in voices that were too high for Emily to understand.

'No doubt you are all wondering about the final competition,' Madame Letsworth began. 'As you know, the Ice Princess is going to have to help to move a fire dragon. To do that, she must perform a magic ice dance for him called the Lulling Dance.'

Several of the girls gasped, but Emily, Molly and Hannah just exchanged looks. They'd already secretly found out about the Lulling Dance the week before and so it wasn't a surprise to them.

'If the magic ice dance works, the dragon will become sleepy and cooperative,' Madame Letsworth continued. 'The Ice Princess will then ask him to leave the mountain. Obviously it is very important that the Ice Princess can skate the Lulling Dance well enough. For this week's competition, you will all perform the dance in front of an audience on Sunday morning.'

Camilla put up her hand. 'Will the best dancer win and be the Ice Princess?'

Madame Letsworth shook her head. 'Not necessarily. The Ice Princess needs to be able to skate the dance accurately, but she also needs to have certain other qualities if she is to make the magic work when she skates in front of the dragon. After watching you all dance and taking into consideration what we have learnt about you during your time here, the teachers and I will draw up a shortlist of three girls before making our final choice. The girl who is then chosen will be presented with a tiara and a pair of silver skates. She will be our Ice Princess.'

Emily felt excited and nervous all at the same time – imagine being chosen as the Ice Princess!

'What will we wear?' asked Molly.

'The Ice Princess always wears a white

dress,' Madame Letsworth replied. 'The
frost fairies will design and make a dress
for each of you to wear for the
competition.' She looked around at them
all. 'I would like you all to practise very
hard this week, girls. It is vitally important
that we choose the right person to be our
Ice Princess to give the Lulling Dance the
best chance of working.'

Emily saw looks of determination on
the faces of everyone around her.

'Now, on to the ice!' Madame Letsworth declared.

They all started warming up. The girls were taught in three groups for skating – beginners, intermediate and advanced. Emily was in the beginners' group with two other girls, Tilda and Heather.

None of them were proper beginners any more. Emily had improved the most and now she could do many of the jumps and spins that the girls in the advanced

group could do, but, even so, she was glad the groups had stayed the same. She really liked her skating teacher, Monsieur Carvallio.

After five minutes, Monsieur Carvallio called them together. He was tall with short dark hair and had pointed ears like all the other ice sylphs. 'As you have just heard, this week you'll be learning the Lulling Dance. It's a difficult dance, but if you try hard, you should all be able to manage it. All three of you have progressed exceptionally well in the last five weeks. Now, let's get started. It begins like this . . .'

Half an hour later, Emily was beginning to understand what Monsieur Carvallio had meant when he had said the dance was difficult. As well as hard jumps like double flips and double toe loops, there were complicated linking steps and spins.

Monsieur Carvallio started by teaching them the first section, which had a double loop jump followed by a fast sequence of steps, and then he let them all practise on their own while he helped them individually.

'This is impossible,' said Tilda to Emily as she fell for the umpteenth time on the double loop.

Emily could manage the jump OK, but she was finding the step sequence that came straight after it hard.

It didn't help that over in the advanced group she could hear Camilla saying loudly, 'Oh, this routine is *so* easy!' To prove her point, she effortlessly turned a double loop and then, just to show off,

leapt into a triple loop, which was even harder. She glanced round smugly.

'Extend your arms more fully, Camilla,' Madame Letsworth said sharply. 'And please concentrate on the routine that you are *supposed* to be learning.'

Emily forced herself to focus on her own skating. She knew that she had to ignore what the others were doing. At the end of the day, all she could do to give herself the best chance of winning the competition was to practise as hard as she could.

Skating backwards, she kicked her left toe into the ice. She pushed upwards with her other leg and spun round twice in the air before landing neatly. *Good*, thought Emily. But as she began on the difficult sequence of fast steps, her skate caught an edge and she landed on the ice with a bump. Emily sighed and got to her feet. It looked like she had a lot of practising to do!

Chapter Three
A Brilliant Idea

Emily worked hard all lesson and
afterwards she stayed on the ice to
practise some more. The rink emptied
until there were just three other people
left – Zoe, Heather and Amanda. They
were all from the Ice Owls dorm. Zoe
was helping Heather, and Amanda was
skating through sections of the routine
on her own.

'Are you staying too?' Emily asked, skating over to Amanda.

When she had first started at the school, Amanda had been really annoying, often boasting and telling tales, as well as being really competitive. But the Ice-skating Academy had been good for her. She seemed to be trying much harder to be nice now.

Amanda nodded. 'Do you want some help?'

'Yes, please,' Emily replied eagerly. 'I'm having a problem with the first section.'

'OK, let me see what you're doing.'

Emily set off. She jumped the double loop and that was fine, but when she started the next steps, her feet seemed to get tangled up and she ended up stopping and exclaiming in frustration.

'You're going too fast,' Amanda told her. 'And you're looking down. It's throwing your balance off. Let's go through it slowly.'

Amanda went through all the steps until Emily could do them properly.

'Wow! Thanks!' she said, amazed Amanda had been so patient.

'No problem.' Amanda smiled. 'You helped me in the scavenger hunt and you really helped Heather last week. Now it's my turn to help you.'

'I wish I could see the dance from start to finish,' Emily said, sighing. 'It might help me to learn it.'

'I could try,' offered Amanda. 'I won't be brilliant, but it'll give you an idea. Why don't you ask the dragons to play the music?'

'It's almost suppertime,' Zoe called to them from across the rink. 'Are you two coming?'

'In a minute,' Amanda called back.

Emily skated over to the large purple music box at the side of the rink and lifted the lid. Inside there was a complicated set of wheels and levers and four pale-blue ice dragons, each about the size of her hand.

'*Hi*,' Emily chirruped in dragon language. '*Would you play the Lulling Dance for us, please?*'

'*Of course,*' one of the dragons chirruped back.

Emily lowered the lid. She loved the ice dragons and had started to learn their language in the second week. She was getting good at it now.

Amanda skated to the centre of the ice.

She stood, hands by her side, one leg
crossed behind the other, waiting for the
beautiful music to begin. Emily watched
as Amanda began to skate through the
routine. She was very good. *Maybe she'll
be the Ice Princess*, Emily thought, watching
as Amanda jumped the double loop
followed by a graceful layback spin, her
dark hair sweeping around her.

Amanda moved into the mid section,
jumping a double flip followed by a

double lutz. Emily rubbed her eyes.
Suddenly she felt really tired. Amanda
was gliding on one leg, lifting the other
leg up behind her. She finished with a
final upright spin. Emily had to blink to
stop her eyes from closing.

Amanda skated over. 'How was that?'
Emily couldn't stop herself. She yawned.

Amanda's face fell. 'Oh, that good.'

'Sorry,' Emily apologized. 'It was great.
I just feel so tired suddenly.'

'Me too,' yawned Zoe, who had been watching from the side with Heather.

'I guess we have had a long skating session,' said Heather, rubbing her eyes.

Amanda looked at the three of them. 'Or . . .' She broke off. 'No, it couldn't be,' she said, shaking her head.

'What?' asked Zoe.

'Well, the dance is supposed to make the dragon sleepy, right?'

Emily stared at her, trying to work out what she was thinking. 'You mean maybe the dance was working? Maybe that's why we're all feeling sleepy!'

'I'm not feeling quite so tired now you've stopped dancing,' said Zoe. 'Just sort of happy and content.'

'Like you've had a long sleep?' said Emily. Zoe nodded.

'Weird! I feel just like that too!' Emily said.

'The magic *must* have been working!' Amanda said in astonishment.

'That's so cool!' breathed Heather.

Emily looked enviously at Amanda. She wished she could dance the routine well enough to make the magic work already. She'd only just managed to do the first section. The girls came off the ice and

Zoe and Heather waited for them while
they changed out of their skates.

'I do love being here,' said Zoe happily.
'All the magic stuff is great – and
learning about the land – but it's also just
amazing being at a school like this. I
always used to read books about boarding
schools and wish I could go. Now I
know what it would be like.'

Emily nodded. 'I wish we'd had a
midnight feast like they do in books.'

'Well, why don't we?' suggested
Amanda. 'We could!'

'Oh, yes!' Zoe gasped. 'We could do it
on Saturday night, our last night here.'

'All of us?' said Emily.

'No, not Camilla,' said Heather
promptly.

'But we can't just leave her out,'

protested Emily. 'That would be really mean.'

Zoe looked thoughtful. 'I suppose we could just have the feast for our two dorms. We don't need to tell anyone in the Snow Foxes dorm.'

'Good idea,' said Heather, pleased. 'Let's do it just for us. And we can have it here. We can eat and skate – perfect!'

'OK,' Zoe said, her eyes shining. 'We meet here at midnight on Saturday night then. Agreed?'

'Agreed!' they all declared.

Emily told her dorm about the feast at suppertime.

'It's a brilliant idea!' exclaimed Molly.

'What will we do about food?' Tilda asked.

'We could ask the frost fairies for some,' suggested Alice.

'We could ask them to join us for the feast too – and the ice dragons,' said Emily eagerly.

'But we'll need to keep it secret from the teachers though,' warned Hannah. 'I bet we'll get into loads of trouble if they find out.'

'And we mustn't let the Snow Foxes know,' muttered Molly, glancing over to where Camilla, Tess, Helena and Clare were sitting at a table together.

Tess saw her looking. 'What are you lot talking about?'

'It's a secret,' they all chorused with grins.

'Oh, ignore them,' said Camilla, turning her back.

Molly giggled, but Emily felt a pang of guilt. She didn't like the Snow Foxes, but it did seem a bit mean to leave them out. 'Maybe we should invite them too?'

'No way!' whispered Molly. 'They'll only spoil it. Now, let's start planning what food to ask the frost fairies for.' Her eyes sparkled. 'This is going to be so much fun!'

Chapter Four
Plans and Preparations

The next morning they had an extra
long lesson with Madame Longley, the
teacher who taught them all about the
magic land. She brought some ice
dragons into the classroom and started
teaching the girls how to speak dragon
language so that the girl chosen to be the
Ice Princess would be able to ask the fire
dragon to leave the mountain.

Emily loved it. She was really good at dragon language already and so she just chatted to Charlie, the smallest ice dragon, while the others tried to work out how to say hello and attempted to ask the dragons to do things.

Some of the girls, like Alice and Hannah, found it easy; others had more trouble. When Camilla asked her ice dragon to fly in a circle, he promptly flew into the waste-paper basket and fell asleep! Emily had to hide her grin. She had a feeling he had understood Camilla very well, but ice dragons could be very mischievous when they wanted to be!

In the skating lesson later that morning, Monsieur Carvallio made them go over the individual jumps in the routine until

Emily's head was spinning. Hannah, Molly, Camilla, Zoe and Amanda, who were all in the advanced group with Madame Letsworth, had already mastered all the different moves.

'You can start linking the sections together now, girls,' Emily heard Madame Letsworth say.

'If we do the whole dance, won't we send each other to sleep?' said Amanda.

Emily had a feeling she was remembering the day before.

'No, I'm sure you will be fine. The dance needs to be skated in a certain way for it to work. If you are just practising for the competition, it is very unlikely you will send anyone to sleep,' Madame Letsworth reassured her. 'But, just in case, don't all do the dance at exactly the same time. The magic is very powerful and the more people who dance it, the stronger it will be.'

Hannah put up her hand. 'If the magic works better when lots of people do it, Madame, why don't we all go and skate the dance for the dragon?' she asked curiously.

'We don't want the dragon to fall asleep, Hannah,' Madame Letsworth reminded her. 'We need him to feel peaceful and happy so that he will listen and agree to move, but if all of you were to dance the Lulling Dance then he would fall asleep completely. That would be disastrous because when fire dragons go to sleep, they sleep for a hundred years. During that time, his breath would melt this land completely.'

Emily saw Monsieur Carvallio glance

at her as she stood listening. She quickly
started skating again. She jumped the
double loop, landed well and followed it
with the step sequence she had been
practising with Amanda the night before.
As she finished it, she felt a surge of
triumph. She'd done it!

'Good work, Emily!' Monsieur
Carvallio called. 'Why don't you start
working on the middle section now? I'll
be over to you in a few minutes.'

45

Emily tried her hardest all lesson. By the end of the class she could manage most of the dance and just had trouble with the final difficult combination of two double jumps followed by a spiral and then a spin.

She fell over quite a few times. But she didn't let herself be put off. *I'll get it right by Sunday*, she thought determinedly. *I will.*

When Emily got off the ice, Camilla was unlacing her skates in the changing area. 'How many bruises have you got, Emily? You must have fallen over about a hundred times today.'

Emily ignored her. Over the last six weeks, she had learnt not to be bothered by Camilla's snide remarks.

'You know, if you skate like that,

you've got absolutely no chance of being the Ice Princess,' Camilla carried on.

'Oh, and *you*'d make such a good one,' Molly said, coming into the changing area. 'At least Emily would be able to talk to the dragon if she was the Ice Princess. If you asked him to leave the mountain, he'd probably not understand you and ask his friends round for a party instead!'

Camilla scowled at Molly. 'I'll learn dragon language by Sunday. It's not that hard. Anyway, you weren't much better!'

'At least my dragon didn't fall asleep,' said Molly.

'Are you coming, Camilla?' Tess called.

'Yeah.' Camilla got up. 'Let's go and talk about *you know what*.' They met each other's eyes and grinned.

'What are you going on about?' Molly asked.

'You lot aren't the only ones with secrets, you know,' Tess said mysteriously.

'It's OK. I'll tell you, Molly,' said Camilla. She leant forward. 'It's . . .' She broke off. 'Nah, sorry,' she said with an infuriating smirk, 'I've changed my mind. See you later!'

Molly rolled her eyes. 'Not if I see you first,' she muttered.

The next few days flew by. There was so much to pack in. Knowing it was her last week in the Land of Ice and Winter, Emily wanted to do all the things she loved best – skiing, taking the huskies out in the woods, sledging and snowball fights.

She also wanted to skate as much as

possible of course. Her practising was paying off and by the end of the week she could perform most of the Lulling Dance well, although she did still have problems with the double–double combination. Everyone else had improved too.

Emily kept watching them and wondering who would be the Ice Princess. Would it be Molly with all her energy, or Hannah with her grace? Camilla, who always seemed to sparkle on the ice, or Amanda, who was so expressive? And there were others who were good too – Zoe, Alice, Tasha.

Or maybe it'll be me, Emily thought, crossing her fingers. She wondered what it would be like to face a fire dragon. It was quite a scary thought, but every night she dreamt about being the Ice Princess.

On Saturday morning Emily woke up
to find the frost fairies had delivered the
girls' costumes in the night. All the girls
had white dresses, but each one was
slightly different. Molly's was dramatic
with a low back and a short, jagged-
edged skirt; Hannah's was longer and
more elegant, made of a velvety material
with long sleeves and a scooped neckline.

Emily thought hers was the most
perfect of all – it had a skirt made of
floaty material, short sleeves, and the neck
and hem were edged with sparkling,
diamond-like jewels. But then everyone
seemed to like their own dress best! The
frost fairies had done really well. The
girls were allowed to wear the costumes
for their morning skating class. It made it
all seem so much more real.

'Really concentrate on yourself and your own performance,' Madame Letsworth told them all before they started. 'This is your last chance for a proper practice.'

Emily had been getting better at the double jump combination followed by the spiral, but she still didn't manage to get it right every time. She thought she had managed it by lunchtime when she had skated the moves ten times without getting them wrong under Monsieur Carvallio's watchful eye. But then, in the afternoon's dress rehearsal, when they took it in turns to skate to the music on their own, she had fallen on the second jump.

Emily got quickly to her feet and carried on, but she was cross with herself.

'Don't worry, it was just one fall,' Hannah said when she skated off the ice.

'Yeah, you did it great this morning, Em,' said Molly.

Emily told herself she hadn't been the only person who had fallen – several of the others had too – but she wished she'd got the routine right.

Hannah squeezed her hand. 'You'll be fine,' she said comfortingly. 'Don't worry.'

Trying to put it behind her, Emily concentrated on clapping and cheering the others as they came off the ice.

As Emily sat down at supper, three of the frost fairies fluttered over. They perched on the table and one of them quickly drew a picture of a plate of cakes on Emily's napkin using magic. She wrote the word 'tonight' underneath it and then pointed at herself and at Emily.

Emily grinned. She'd been so busy skating, she hadn't really thought about the midnight feast all day, but it was only a few hours away now. 'Yes, tonight,' she whispered.

The fairies giggled in delight and flew away. They seemed just as excited by the idea as Emily.

Hannah, Molly, Tilda and Alice came to sit down with their food. 'I can't wait until tonight,' whispered Tilda.

'The frost fairies have said they'll wake us up,' said Molly, who'd been organizing the feast.

'I'm not going to need waking up,' said Alice. 'There's no way I'm going to be able to sleep.'

'Me neither,' said Emily.

But, by the time they went to bed,

they were all so tired after the busy day that they fell fast asleep within five minutes. Emily was in the middle of a dream about skating in front of an ice monster when she felt something tickling her face. She sat up. It was dark and two frost fairies were fluttering in front of her. Emily blinked as everything came flooding back. Of course! It was time for the midnight feast!

Chapter Five
Midnight Magic

Within a few minutes everyone was awake. 'Come on!' hissed Molly.

Alice giggled. 'This is brilliant!'

'We've got to be really quiet,' said Hannah. 'We mustn't let any of the teachers hear us.'

Putting on their dressing gowns, they crept downstairs to the corridor where the Snow Foxes and Ice Owls had their dorms. As they tiptoed past the Snow Foxes dorm, Emily bit her lip. The Snow Foxes, particularly Camilla, were very annoying, but it felt a bit strange to be doing something big and exciting at the school without them.

The Ice Owls were waiting. They all hurried down the final flight of stairs and along the deserted corridors towards the kitchen. The frost fairies flew in front, leading the way.

The kitchen was a massive room painted a sunshine yellow, with three large tables and a huge cooker. Bunches of dried flowers and herbs hung from the ceiling and frost fairies swooped around. On one of the tables a wonderful feast was laid out – iced biscuits in the shape of skates, pink cupcakes, scones, a massive bowl of strawberries and jugs of fruit juice. Emily grinned. This was going to be the best midnight feast ever!

Everyone picked up a jug or a plate and carried it to the ice rink. They started whispering in excitement.

'Shh!' said Hannah quickly as they reached the bottom of the staircase that led up to the teachers' rooms.

One of the frost fairies flew away up the stairs. 'The fairies are going to take it in turns to keep watch in case the teachers wake up,' Molly whispered.

They reached the rink. The moon and stars were shining down through the glass roof and the ice was glittering with a silvery glow. All the dragons who worked at the school were there, perched on top of the music box. They waved as the girls came in, and the smallest one, Charlie, turned a somersault.

The frost fairies spread out a snowy-white tablecloth on one of the square benches and everyone put down the food and drink. Molly made sure the heavy doors were shut properly so no noise would carry up to the teachers.

Emily glanced at the rink. It looked beautiful in the moonlight. 'Let's skate before eating.'

The ice dragons jumped into the music box and almost immediately a lively tune flooded out. Everyone changed into their skates and started to whizz round, gliding in circles, jumping and spinning. After a week of practising just one dance, it was lovely to be able to skate however they wanted.

Emily sped up and pushed off, arms tight to her chest as she spun round in the air before landing on one leg with her arms out. Skating on, she turned into a spin on one leg. She whizzed round before finally stopping and her body felt like it was glowing. She grinned.

'Come on, it's time for the feast!' called Molly at last.

They all skated over to the entrance.
But, just as they were getting off the ice,
the doors of the ice rink opened!
Everyone caught their breath and froze.
Then Camilla, Tess, Helena and Clare
walked in. For a moment the two sets of
girls just stared at each other. The Snow
Foxes looked just as surprised as Emily
and her friends.

'What are you all doing here?'
demanded Camilla.

'They're having a feast!' exclaimed Tess,
pointing at the food.

'So what if we are? Why are you here?'
said Molly.

'We thought it would be fun to have a
midnight skate and play some games on
the last night,' said Camilla. 'We've been
planning it all week.' She stared at the

food. 'So you've been planning a midnight feast?' Her usual smugness seemed to be replaced by complete surprise.

Molly nodded. 'We've been planning it all week too.'

'So what do we do now?' Tess said.

Amanda frowned. 'You lot can go away. We were here first.'

Camilla raised her eyebrows. 'So?'

'I know!' Emily burst in. 'Why don't we all just do something together?' She looked round at the others. 'There's loads of food. They can join in and then we can play games. It'll be fun and, after all, it is our last night here. Tomorrow we'll be going home.'

Camilla, Tess, Molly and Amanda all started to protest loudly.

'Shh!' said Hannah in alarm. 'The doors are still open!'

A frost fairy came whizzing down the corridor. She flew over the Snow Foxes' heads, chattering at the other fairies. They all squeaked in alarm.

'What's the matter?' demanded Molly.

The ice dragons chirruped and Emily immediately understood.

'Oh, no!' she gasped. 'The frost fairy

said that the noise has woken Madame Letsworth up! She might come down from her bedroom.'

'What are we going to do?' gasped Alice.

'We're going to be in so much trouble!' said Molly.

'And not just us but the frost fairies and dragons too,' added Hannah.

Emily racked her brains. They couldn't let that happen. But what could they do?

'I know!' gasped Camilla. 'The Lulling Dance! You've all got your skates on. Do that!'

Emily stared at her. 'You mean dance it and try and send Madame Letsworth back to sleep?'

'Yes, Madame Letsworth told us it

works if you even just think about the person you're trying to send to sleep. Provided they are nearby, they don't have to be actually watching it,' said Camilla.

'And the more people that do it, the more powerful the magic is,' Hannah reminded them. 'That's a brilliant idea, Camilla. Come on!'

The frost fairy who had warned them raced back to Madame Letsworth's room to check what was happening. The dragons dived inside the music box. Within seconds, the beautiful, soothing music of the Lulling Dance was flowing out across the rink.

Emily counted herself in. At the same moment as all the others, she started to dance. She fixed the thought of Madame Letsworth in her mind. It would be awful if everyone got into trouble — not just them but the frost fairies and ice dragons too.

She pushed into the double loop. As she landed, she heard the sound of everyone else landing too. They skated on until they came to the final combination. Emily felt herself tense. Would she fall again as she had that afternoon? She took off and spun through the air. She landed badly on the second jump and stumbled, but didn't fall.

Regaining her balance, Emily quickly joined in with the final glide and spin. She tried not to think about it. It didn't matter how she did herself; she just hoped enough people were doing the dance well enough for its magic to work.

They finished and all stared at the

doorway, holding their breath. Camilla and the other Snow Foxes looked anxiously down the corridor. Had the dance worked?

After a few minutes, the frost fairy came flying back. She was squeaking excitedly, her little head nodding. Everyone let out their breath in a rush.

'We did it!' gasped Molly. Camilla hastily shut the doors as everyone started to exclaim and talk.

The frost fairy who had just arrived was chattering with the other fairies. The ice dragons listened in and then started chirruping.

'She went back to sleep,' Emily interpreted. 'Phew!'

Molly looked at Camilla. 'It was a really good idea to do the dance. Thanks.

Look, do you want to join in with the feast? Emily was right. We can all have a good time together.'

Camilla's face broke into a smile. 'OK. Cool!'

They ate every bit of food with the dragons and the fairies joining in. Afterwards the girls all skated, with the fairies zipping round them and the

dragons taking it in turns to play the
music and flap around.

It was brilliant fun. No one argued and
not even Camilla was mean. She
suggested some really good games for
them all to play and organized them into
teams. Emily went to bed feeling very
happy. It had been even better than she
had expected.

And it's the competition tomorrow, she
thought. For a moment, she remembered
how she had stumbled in the dance that
night. What if that happened in the
competition? She pushed the thought
away, making herself think about the Ice
Princess. This time tomorrow they
would know who she was going to be.
Emily hugged her arms around her chest.

Oh, please, she prayed. *Please let it be me!*

Chapter Six
The Final Competition

By eleven o'clock the next morning the
area around the ice rink was crowded with
ice sylphs. They had arrived on sledges and
sleighs pulled by reindeer and huskies.
There was a buzz of excited chatter as they
settled into their seats and as the teachers
took their places behind a long table.

Unlike the other skating competitions,
where the three skating teachers had

been the only judges, for this final competition *all* the teachers who taught at the school were involved.

Emily and the others waited in the changing area. They were allowed to wear make-up for the competitions so Emily had put on some glittering silver eyeshadow and mascara to darken her eyelashes. Hannah had helped her fix her hair back in a bun and then Emily had put in some sparkling white clips.

She went to the barrier. The surface of the ice was shining. No one would ever have been able to guess there had been a midnight feast the night before!

'I can't believe this is our last competition here,' said Molly, coming over. 'I wish we could come back.'

Emily nodded. Her chest felt tight as if

she couldn't really breathe. *This is it*, she thought. *This is what we've been waiting for, for six weeks. The Ice Princess is going to be chosen!*

She thought about everything they had done since coming to the Land of Ice and Winter, the lessons they had been to, the tricks Molly had played, the fun and excitement they'd had. There was the time they had rescued Alice from the ice monster; the scavenger hunt when they had been out in the land; there was the week Emily had looked after Molly after she'd hurt her ankle; and then the time Emily had had to stop an out–of–control sledge pulled by huskies. So many things had happened to her!

Madame Letsworth stood up and a hush fell. 'Welcome, everybody! As you

know, today we will choose the Ice
Princess. For this final competition, all
the girls will skate the Lulling Dance.
First to go will be Zoe Hunter!'

'Good luck!' the girls whispered to
Zoe as she stepped on to the ice. Even
Camilla and the other Snow Foxes joined
in. After the night before, they had been
much friendlier and right now they all
seemed just as nervous as each other.

Zoe skated towards the centre of the rink, took her position and the music started.

It was a brilliant opening dance. Zoe was a really good skater, but she didn't have the natural elegance of Hannah or Camilla or the drama of Molly and Amanda. However, this time she threw herself into it – her jumps and spins keeping in perfect time to the music. When she finished, she was beaming.

She skated off to loud applause and collapsed on to the bench, looking very relieved as the others crowded round to congratulate her.

One after the other, the girls went on to the ice. Some, like Tilda, Helena and Alice, fell or stumbled. Heather fell twice with nerves. Others, like Zoe and

Amanda, hardly made a single mistake. No matter how they did though, there were always girls waiting to crowd round them and hug them and tell them they had been brilliant. Everyone's differences seemed to have been forgotten in the excitement of the day.

Emily could hardly bear to watch when it was Molly and Hannah's turns. But she needn't have worried. They both did really well. Molly whizzed around the ice with her usual dash and sparkle, leaping higher than anyone else had, and Hannah skated beautifully, getting a particularly loud round of applause as she finished.

'That was brilliant!' cried Emily as Hannah came off. 'Oh, help – it's me next!' Her heart was beating fast.

'You can do it, Em!' called Molly.

'And now we have Emily Walker!'
Madame Letsworth announced.

Emily stepped on to the ice and glided
to her starting position. She crossed one
leg behind the other. The music started
and she was off! First the circle of
backward crossovers and then the double
loop. She landed it perfectly and skated
on.

Move followed move until she reached
the double combination. She spun over
the ice in her double flip, but, as she
lifted off for the double lutz, Emily knew
she hadn't got enough height. She landed
off balance. Her arms flailed and the next
moment she was falling onto the ice, her
hip banging into the cold, hard surface.

She'd fallen!

But even while she was thinking it, she

was getting to her feet. The music was carrying on and she knew she had to as well. Trying to put the fall behind her, Emily began the glide and then turned into the final spin. She twirled round and round and then stopped on beat with the music, her hands down.

Smile, she told herself fiercely. And she managed to, although she could feel the tears prickling at the back of her eyes. She'd fallen over. She was never going to be the Ice Princess now. But Emily wouldn't let herself cry on the ice. She bowed to the audience and then skated off, her head held high, her smile never wavering.

'Oh, Em!' Molly said, hugging her as Emily stepped off the ice and suddenly gave way to the tears.

'It doesn't matter,' said Hannah, stroking her back as Emily sobbed.

'You were brilliant. It was just one fall,' said Amanda.

'I fell twice,' Heather put in.

Emily fought back her tears. She knew how upset her friends were to see her crying. Scrubbing her hands over her face, she swallowed hard. But whatever they said, she knew the truth. She'd fallen and now she wouldn't get to be the Ice Princess. Lots of people had skated perfectly.

Camilla, the last person to go, skated on. Emily watched numbly as Camilla performed the routine with her usual confidence. As she came off, Emily forced herself to congratulate her. 'That was a fantastic routine. Well done!'

'Thanks!' Camilla said, her eyes glowing. 'I'm sorry you fell.' And for once she sounded like she genuinely meant it. Emily gave a small smile and turned away.

The judges got together to discuss who should be on the shortlist. Everyone waited nervously. Zoe bit her nails and Amanda fiddled with her hair. Camilla paced up and down while Emily gripped Molly and Hannah's hands. She hoped they would be chosen even if she wouldn't be now.

Finally all the judges sat back down, leaving Madame Letsworth standing. Emily held her breath. Who was going to be on the shortlist to be the Ice Princess?

Chapter Seven
The Shortlist

'Well done, girls,' Madame Letsworth said. 'You all skated extremely well.' The audience applauded in agreement. 'We have now reached our decision about the three girls who are on the shortlist,' she continued. 'We have been watching you all carefully over the last six weeks and we have drawn the shortlist up not just on today's performance, but taking into account what we have learnt about you in your time here. As I have told you before, it is vitally important that the person who is chosen to be the Ice Princess has certain qualities. She must be brave, for it will take courage to face the dragon; she must care deeply about the land; and, most importantly, if she is to make the dance work, she must have a kind, true heart. The chosen girls are . . .'

The whole world seemed to hold its breath. Emily's heart thudded. After everything Madame Letsworth had just said, did she still have a chance?

Oh, please, please, please, she prayed.

The silence seemed to go on forever and then Madame Letsworth spoke: 'Hannah Peters, Zoe Hunter and Emily Walker!'

Emily blinked, unable to take it in.
Around her she heard a mixture of
excited gasps and disappointed sighs.

'Oh, wow!' Molly whispered. 'That's
brilliant! Both of you!'

Emily was lost for words. 'I can't
believe it! After the competition, I never
imagined . . . I thought there was no way
. . .' She broke off as it began to sink in.

'I wish you were on the shortlist too, Molly!' Hannah said.

'So do I,' sighed Molly. 'But I'm really glad you two are,' she added generously and hugged them both. 'Really, really glad.'

'Thanks,' said Emily. She knew she'd have found it really hard if Molly and Hannah had been chosen and not her. She gave Molly a tight hug back. 'You're brilliant.'

Madame Letsworth called for quiet and announced that there would be lunch in the hall for the girls. 'The other teachers and I are now going away to decide who the Ice Princess will be and we will tell you in an hour's time,' she said. 'Until then, try and relax.'

★

There was a delicious lunch of salads, fresh bread, cheese and cold meats laid out in the hall, but Emily couldn't eat a thing. Everyone, even Camilla, had congratulated her and she walked up and down the room unable to think about anything but being the Ice Princess.

Hannah and Zoe joined her. 'This waiting is awful,' said Zoe.

'Just think, this afternoon, one of us will be dancing in front of a dragon!' Hannah breathed.

'And if we don't get it right, he won't move,' said Emily.

'If we do get it right, we can make a wish,' Zoe reminded her.

But Emily couldn't think about wishes yet. She was torn between hoping desperately to be chosen as the Ice

Princess and yet not wanting Hannah or Zoe to be disappointed. *Oh, goodness*, she thought. *Which of us is it going to be?*

An hour later, Madame Letsworth came in with the other teachers. She clapped her hands. 'Hannah, Zoe and Emily, would you come here, please?' The three girls walked over anxiously.

'Before we go to the rink and make the official announcement, we wanted to come and talk to you first. We have a problem.' Madame Letsworth looked serious.

'We have been discussing which of you should be the Ice Princess, but we simply cannot decide – the votes are evenly divided. All of you skated very well today. Yes, Emily had a fall, but

Monsieur Carvallio and I have full confidence that she can perform the routine. Madame Longley says that you are all capable of speaking the dragon language needed, and over the last few weeks all three of you have shown that you are kind, helpful and brave.

'It seems impossible to choose between you. We have decided we will talk about it a little more, but I wanted to let you know that, at the moment, we are considering having all three of you as Ice Princesses.'

All three of us! Emily's heart leapt. She saw Hannah and Zoe grin. Behind them there was a buzz of excited chatter from the others.

Oh, wow! We'll all be the Ice Princess, Emily thought in delight. *We'll all get to do the dance and talk to the dragon . . .*

And then she remembered something Madame Letsworth had said earlier in the week: *'The magic is very powerful and the more people who dance it, the stronger it will be . . . if all of you were to dance the Lulling Dance then the dragon would fall asleep completely.'*

Emily put up her hand. 'But you told us that the dragon might go to sleep for a

hundred years if lots of people skated the dance.'

Madame Letsworth looked grave. 'There is that danger. The other teachers and I hope that it will not happen if there are just three of you. But if the dance did send the dragon to sleep then it would be a disaster for the land – for all of us.'

Emily stared at her.

'Now, you have five minutes, girls,' Madame Letsworth said. 'The teachers and I are going to discuss it one last time.'

Emily took a step back. She couldn't stop thinking over the headteacher's words. Madame Letsworth had said she hoped the dragon wouldn't fall asleep if three of them danced. *But what if he does?* worried Emily.

She wanted to be on her own to think.

Hurrying out of the room, she went to the back door. Slipping through it, she took a deep breath of the cold air. The snowy gardens stretched out, leading to the glittering frozen lake. Behind the lake were the woods and the High Mountains. It was all so beautiful. If the dragon continued to sleep, this would all be destroyed.

I can't let that happen, thought Emily unhappily. *We mustn't risk it.*

A wave of sadness welled up inside her. She wanted to be the Ice Princess so much, but the land mattered more. Suddenly she knew what she had to do and, taking another deep breath, she went back inside.

Chapter Eight
The Ice Princess

Emily went into the hall and walked over to Madame Letsworth. The other girls were all clustered together, talking excitedly.

'Yes, Emily?' the headteacher said.

'I . . . I don't want to be one of the Ice Princesses, Madame.' Emily's words came out in a rush. 'Hannah and Zoe can do it on their own. If there's just two of them, there's less chance the dragon will go to sleep.'

Madame Letsworth studied her. 'You mean you'd really give up being the Ice Princess just to give the Lulling Dance a better chance of working?'

Emily swallowed and nodded. 'I want to be the Ice Princess, I really do, but I want the land to be OK even more.'

'Then this changes things. Wait here a moment.' Madame Letsworth had a quick word with Madame Li and then looked round. 'Hannah! Zoe! Can we talk in my office, please?'

Hannah, Zoe and Emily followed Madame Letsworth out of the hall. Hannah and Zoe shot Emily puzzled looks, but she was just as confused as them. When they got to the office,

Madame Letsworth shut the door. 'Emily has just come to me and said that she would rather not dance. She is worried that the dance will send the dragon to sleep if all three of you skate it.'

'I just don't want to risk it not working,' Emily told the others.

'That's really unselfish, Em,' Hannah said slowly.

Zoe looked guilty. 'Yeah.'

'It would probably be best if just one of us went, wouldn't it?' Hannah said to Madame Letsworth. The headteacher nodded.

'I won't go,' Hannah and Zoe said at the same time.

Madame Letsworth raised her eyebrows. 'Someone has to.'

'Then it should be Emily,' Hannah put in. 'After all, she was the one who put the land first and was the first to say she wouldn't go.'

Emily stared. 'But, Hannah, that wouldn't be fair –'

'Em! We can't all be the Ice Princess, even though we'd like to,' Zoe interrupted her. 'It has to be just one. I agree with Hannah. I think it should be you.'

'Your friends are right, Emily,' Madame Letsworth said. 'You should be the Ice Princess. The way you responded just now has proved it to me. The Lulling Dance must not be performed for the person's own glory or benefit; the magic in it will only work if it is skated completely unselfishly. Did you ever wonder why we needed a human girl to do it – why one of us didn't just skate the dance?'

Emily nodded.

'No ice sylph can skate it because any ice sylph would be dancing to save their own land and home,' Madame Letsworth explained. 'Magic in this land comes from unselfish acts, which is why we need a human girl to be our Ice Princess: someone who will dance simply to save

the land because she has come to love it.
Out of the three of you, you were the first
to show a willingness to sacrifice your
own happiness in order to help our land.
And that means, Emily, you truly are the
right person to be the Ice Princess.'

Zoe nodded and Hannah squeezed
Emily's hand. 'You *are*.'

Madame Letsworth looked between
the three of them. 'This is why the dance
hasn't sent people to sleep this week. You
have all been skating the dance over and
over. Yet because you have all been
practising it to try and win the
competition for yourselves, the magic has
not worked and so no one has become
sleepy.'

'It did work a few times,' said Zoe.

'Only when it was being performed

unselfishly, maybe to help someone else
or to stop others getting into trouble.'
Madame Letsworth's eyes twinkled. 'It is
probably just as well for all of you that
teachers, unlike dragons, do not fall
asleep for a hundred years!'

Emily stared at their headteacher.

'You knew about the feast?' Zoe
exclaimed.

'I know most of the things that happen
in this school, Zoe. I am glad you all had
a good time,' Madame Letsworth said
with a smile. 'Now, let us go to the rink
and tell everyone the decision that has
been made.'

The rink was still crowded with people.
All the other girls were there and the
teachers had joined them. When

Madame Letsworth announced that
Emily was to be the Ice Princess, Emily
saw the surprised looks on the others'
faces. 'Don't worry, we'll explain to
them what happened,' Zoe whispered.

Madame Letsworth presented Zoe and
Hannah with a pair of sparkling silver
skates each as runners-up and then it was
Emily's turn. The audience applauded
loudly as Madame Letsworth presented

her with her skates and then opened a
box and took out a delicate crystal tiara.

'You are the Ice Princess, Emily.'
Madame Letsworth placed the sparkling
tiara on her head. 'Well done,' she said
with a warm smile as the audience all
clapped and cheered. 'Now it is time to
see if you can make the Lulling Dance
work.'

Emily, the other girls and the teachers all
set off for the High Mountains in sledges
pulled by teams of huskies. The girls
were wrapped up in fur rugs, most of
them chattering excitedly. Emily was
quiet with nerves. *What if I can't do the
dance*, she thought anxiously. *What if the
magic doesn't work? What if I fail and the
land continues to melt?*

Hannah looked at her sympathetically, reading her mind. 'You'll be able to do it, Em.'

'Yeah,' said Molly, squeezing her hand. 'You'll be brilliant!'

Emily gave them a grateful look. 'Thanks.' She swallowed. Her stomach felt full of fluttering butterflies, but she was very glad she had Molly and Hannah there with her.

At last, the sledges came to a halt by a large glittering lake.

'Look!' exclaimed Molly.

Emily caught her breath. The High Mountains rose up behind the lake's frozen surface. Coiled around the top of one of the mountains was an enormous dark-red dragon. His giant wings were folded flat against his sides and his long

spiky tail was wound round the
mountain top. As he breathed in and out,
jets of fire streamed from his nostrils.
Emily stared. This was it – the moment
when everyone found out if she was the
right person to be the Ice Princess.

'We'll have to stop here,' said Trakin, the
ice sylph who was driving Emily's sledge.
'This lake is the closest to the dragon that
we can go. Further on, everywhere is
starting to melt. Skate the Lulling Dance
and, if the magic works, he will fly down
from the mountain top and then you can
talk to him and ask him to leave.'

Emily got off the sledge, her heart
beating fast. Everyone else started to pile
off too. She felt very nervous as they all
looked at her expectantly.

Monsieur Carvallio unloaded a music

box from his sledge. Two ice dragons popped their heads out and waved at Emily and she immediately felt a little better.

'Put your skates on,' Madame Letsworth told her gently.

'Good luck!' whispered Hannah, and Molly gave her a last hug.

'Think about the dragon, Emily,' Madame Letsworth told her as she stepped on to the ice. 'And dance for the land. You can do this.'

Emily looked at all her friends who were gathered round and then she gazed at the beautiful mountains. Skating on to the river, she took her starting position. Pictures of the Land of Ice and Winter flowed through her mind: everything she had seen and done in the last six weeks, the wonderful creatures, the beautiful scenery, the kind ice sylphs.

The music started and Emily began to dance. She glided, jumped and spun in a way she had only ever dreamt of before she came to this magical land – she almost felt like she was becoming part of the music. It carried her through the routine, surging beneath her as she thought about the dragon.

Emily didn't think about falling over even once. She just skated with all her heart and soul, even through the difficult combination. Reaching the final spin, the world blurred around her and Emily breathlessly came to a stop to the sound of everyone clapping. But that was drowned out by a different noise – the sound of great wings beating in the air.

A shadow fell over the lake and Emily gasped as the dragon flew down from the mountain. He landed on the ice, his vast red bulk filling the lake. For a moment she felt very scared, but she fought the urge to run. The dragon's large, dark eyes were curious but peaceful.

Emily cleared her throat. 'Um, *hello*,' she said in dragon language.

The dragon stared at her. '*What do you want, human child?*' His voice rumbled out, shaking the air.

'*I'm here to ask you to leave this land. Your breath is warming everything up. It's going to cause great floods. Please will you move on?*' Emily asked.

The dragon stared down at her. '*I am really melting the land?*'

'*Yes*,' Emily told him. '*If you stay here,*

the whole land will be destroyed.'

The dragon thought about it for a long moment. *'I like it in these mountains, but I am rested now. Very well, I will move on.'* He blew out a stream of flames from his nostrils, the heat scorching Emily's skin. *'I liked your dance, child.'*

Emily smiled at him. *'Thank you. I did it for you.'*

The dragon stretched out his giant wings. He flapped them three times and then took off into the sky.

Emily heard the others gasp. Madame Letsworth came skating on to the lake.

'He's going!' Emily said in astonishment. She couldn't quite believe it. She had thought it was going to be so much harder.

Madame Letsworth smiled. 'Because of the magic of the dance. Well done, Emily. Now, quickly. Make your wish. You have created magic here by doing the Lulling Dance. While the magic lingers, whatever you wish for will be granted.'

'I've got to decide already?' Emily hadn't even thought about it properly.

'Yes, but be quick. You must make your wish before the magic fades.'

Emily's mind raced. There were so many things . . . Her eyes fell on Hannah and Molly. They grinned and waved. Suddenly something Molly had said during the competition came back to Emily. Of course! It was perfect!

'I wish . . .' she began.

'In your head, Emily,' Madame Letsworth said warningly. 'You must not speak a wish aloud.'

Emily nodded and said the wish in her head. As she finished, she felt a tingle run through her and suddenly the lake lit up with glowing lines.

'That's where I skated!' Emily exclaimed, looking at the shining carvings on the ice.

'Yes. It means the magic is working. Your wish will be granted.' Madame

Letsworth's eyes met Emily's and Emily had the strangest feeling that the headteacher knew what she had wished for. But then she knew so many things!

The glittering lines slowly faded and the dragon soared away overhead.

'Come, let us rejoin the others,' said Madame Letsworth.

Smiling happily, Emily skated over to meet her friends.

Chapter Nine
Going Home

'I can't believe we're about to go home,' said Molly.

Emily nodded. 'I know.' It seemed impossible that very soon their time at skating school would be over. She still almost couldn't believe she had got to be the Ice Princess, but she knew that the memory of dancing for the dragon would live with her forever.

'I'm going to miss everyone so much,' sighed Hannah.

A massive party had been laid on for them in the hall when they got back. The table was piled high with food, and the frost fairies had hung streamers around the room. Everyone had a great time and, after all the food was eaten, the teachers gave them each silver charm bracelets from which hung a pair of white enamel skates. Anyone who had won a pair of coloured skates also had tiny skates of the same colour.

Emily had four charms – more than anyone else. 'I wish that we could take the real skates back,' she said, touching the charms.

'They'd be a bit hard to explain!' said Hannah.

'Maybe you should have made that your wish,' said Molly. She looked at Emily curiously. 'So, what *did* you wish for?'

Emily shook her head. 'I'll tell you later.' She wanted to hold on to her secret for a little longer. She went to the window and looked out at the gardens. It had been such an amazing six weeks.

Two frost fairies fluttered over and landed on her shoulders. They touched her cheeks with their tiny hands and chattered softly. 'I'll miss you,' Emily told them. 'I'll miss everything here – the dragons, you, the teachers, the classes. Everything.' But now she had made her wish, her heart didn't feel quite so heavy.

Madame Letsworth clapped her hands. 'I'm afraid it is time for you to leave for home now, girls.'

There was a chorus of gasps.

'Not now!'

'Can't we stay just a little longer?'

'Just one more night?'

Madame Letsworth shook her head. 'No, I'm afraid not. Your time here is over. You must return to your family and friends. Take the lessons you have learnt and your memories with you, but remember, do not speak of anything that has happened here to anyone who does not know of this land or your memories will fade and then you will never come back.'

'You mean we *might* come back?' said Molly eagerly.

'Maybe.' Madame Letsworth's eyes met Emily's and she smiled. 'Now, say your goodbyes and get into a circle.'

The girls quickly started hugging each other. 'Bye!' Amanda and Heather cried to Emily.

'Bye!' gasped Emily. Turning, she came face to face with Camilla.

'See you,' Camilla said and for a moment her mouth flickered into a smile. 'It's been fun.'

Emily smiled back. 'Yes. It has.'

She was swept away into a whirl of saying goodbye to Tilda and Alice and the others, and then Hannah and Molly grabbed her hands.

'I can't believe this is it! Friends forever?' said Molly. 'Wherever we are.'

Hannah and Emily both nodded.

'And we will come back. Don't worry,' Emily said quickly. 'It'll be OK.'

Molly frowned. 'Was that your wish?'

Emily nodded. 'Yes, I said –' But before she could say any more, Madame Letsworth was giving them instructions.

'On the count of three, take hold of the white skates on your charm bracelets, girls. One, two . . .'

'See you soon!' Emily whispered frantically to Hannah and Molly. 'I promise.'

'. . . Three!'

Emily's fingers closed around the white charm on the bracelet and the next second she felt herself spinning round and round as if she was on the ice. Faster and faster she went until the world blurred into a sparkling cloud around her. Then suddenly her feet landed with a bump.

Even before Emily opened her eyes she

knew she wasn't standing in the school any more. There was grass beneath her feet, birds calling and the faint sound of a radio. She opened her eyes. She was back in the garden of her house! The charms on the bracelet jingled slightly together.

I'm home, Emily thought.

Happiness and sadness swept over her at the same time. She looked around the garden and imagined her friends all arriving back in their own lives too.

But we'll see each other again, she thought quickly.

The words of her wish echoed back to her: *I wish that everyone who wants to can come back to stay at the school next year.*

Yes. They would go back. The magic *would* make it happen.

The back door opened. 'Mum!' cried

Emily, her heart doing a double flip. She ran over and threw her arms around her mum. It seemed forever since she had last seen her, even though she knew that to her mum it would only have been five minutes ago. 'I love you!'

Laughing at her enthusiasm, her mum hugged her back. 'I love you too, sweetheart. And guess what? I've got some good news. Dad just phoned. He's going to be home from his work trip early so that means I'll be able to take you skating at the weekend after all. I thought we could go out on Saturday, just you and me. We could go skating and then have lunch.'

Emily imagined going to the local rink. What would her mum say when she saw how well she could skate now?

She'd have to be careful not to be too
good or her mum would completely
freak!

'So, what do you think?' Mrs Walker
asked eagerly.

Emily grinned. 'I think you're the best
mum in the world!'

She hugged her mum more tightly.
She'd had an amazing time in the Land
of Ice and Winter, but it was lovely to be
home, particularly knowing that,
although her adventures in the land were
over for now, they weren't over forever.
One day, she would go back to the
Magic Ice-skating Academy and see all
her friends. One day, the magic would
whisk her away again.

One day, Emily thought with a smile.

Do you dream of becoming an Ice Princess?

Have you ever wanted to go to a REAL Skating School?

All readers of *Skating School* get FREE membership to the National Ice Skating Association's Skate UK programme!

Skate UK will help you to learn all the moves and basic skills
you need to become a true Ice Princess! It's all about fun
and continuous movement and is taught in groups,
so why not share your love of *Skating School* with
your friends and bring them too?

To get your free membership, go to
www.iceskating.org.uk/skatingschool
and enter the secret password: **Twirl**.

Skate UK is taught by licensed NISA coaches and can be
assisted by trained Programme Assistants.

For full terms and conditions visit:

www.lindachapman.co.uk

www.iceskating.org.uk/skatingschool

Do you want to enter super competitions,
get sneak previews and download lots of
Skating School fun?

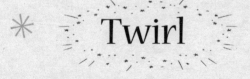

Get YOUR skates on
join the
Sparkle Club
today!
lindachapman.co.uk

Just enter this secret password:

Twirl

The Land of Ice and Winter is waiting for you ...

Design your own ice-skating dress!

The tiny frost fairies have been working overtime designing the beautiful dresses for the girls to wear in the Ice-skating Academy competitions.

Using this dress as a template, the fairies need you to draw the most magical ice-skating outfit you can think of. Every month one lucky winner will receive a magical *Skating School* goody bag!

Send your drawing

with your name and address to:

Skating School Competition, Puffin Marketing, 80 Strand, London WC2R 0RL

Or e-mail them to: **skatingschool@uk.penguingroup.com**

Welcome back to the magical Land of Ice and Winter
… a world where all your dreams come true!

A brand-new *Skating School* series

Coming soon!

Hi there,

I hope you've enjoyed reading about the adventures of the girls who go to the Magic Ice-skating Academy. I love writing them all down! Wouldn't it be amazing to go to the Land of Ice and Winter and see all the creatures who live there? Can you imagine holding an actual ice dragon or talking to a frost fairy?

Sometimes readers write to me and ask about my life. Being a writer is the best job ever. I live in a cottage in a village with my family and two dogs – a Bernese mountain dog and a golden retriever. I spend my days writing and going to visit schools and libraries to talk about writing.

I always think I'm really lucky because I get to spend my days writing about magic – mermaids, unicorns, stardust spirits, genies and now the Land of Ice and Winter. If you love them too then why not go to **www.lindachapman.co.uk** and join the Sparkle Club? It's my online fan club with loads of activities and downloads, and you can only get to it by using the secret password at the back of this book. Have fun!

Love,

Linda
xxx